The Three Horrid Little Pigs

This book is dedicated to Claudia and Kate (and long-suffering moms everywhere) –L.P.

tiger tales

5 River Road, Suite 128, Wilton, CT 06897
This edition published in the United States 2018
First paperback edition (978-1-58925-423-7) published in the United States 2010
First hardcover edition (978-1-58925-077-2) published in the United States 2008
Originally published in Great Britain 2008
by Little Tiger Press
Text and illustrations copyright © 2008, 2018 Liz Pichon
ISBN-13: 978-1-68010-109-6
ISBN-10: 1-68010-109-9
Printed in China
LTP/1400/2213/0318

For more insight and activities, visit us at
www.tigertalesbooks.com

The Three Horrid Little Pigs

by Liz Pichon

tiger tales

Once upon a time, three horrid little pigs lived with their mother in a tiny house.

The little pigs were very bad, and they drove their mother crazy!

"I've had enough of you pesky pigs," she told them. "It's about time you moved out and made your own way in the world!"

So she packed their bags and sent them away.

OUT!

Stop pushing!

The first horrid little pig came across a big pile of straw. "This straw is PERFECT for me to build my house," he said.

But the little pig was lazy, and he didn't make his straw house very strong at all.

Luckily, a big friendly wolf (who just happened to be a builder) was passing by.

"Good grief!" said the wolf. "What a mess that house is. I'll see if I can help."

"Little pig, little pig, may I come in?" asked the wolf. "NO WAY!" shouted the pig. "Not by the hairs of my chinny chin chin will I let a WOLF in!

Put one paw on my house

Oh, dear!

and I'll **huff**, and I'll **puff**, and I'll

KICK YOU OUT!"

"I only wanted to help," said the wolf sadly
as he went on his way.

The second horrid
little pig found a
huge pile
of twigs.
"These twigs
will make a great house
for me!" he exclaimed.
But the little pig
was even lazier
than his brother...

. . . so the house was a disaster!

When the friendly wolf saw the terrible tangle of twigs, he thought, *Oh, no! That house is an accident waiting to happen. I'd better help.*

Oh my goodness!

"Little pig, little pig, may I come in?" asked the wolf.

"GET LOST!" shouted the rude little pig. "Not by the hairs of my chinny chin chin will I let a WOLF in!

Put one paw on my house and I'll **huff**,

and I'll **puff,**

and I'll

THROW

YOU

RIGHT

OUT!"

"I'm sorry," said the wolf.
"I only wanted to help."

How rude!

The third horrid little pig was SO lazy, he couldn't be bothered to build a house at all. So he found a nice chicken coop instead...and moved in.

The friendly wolf just happened to be nearby.

Oh, my! he thought. *Those poor chickens! I must speak to that pig.*

Pig stole our house!

HELP!

"Little pig, little pig, may I come in?"
"SCRAM!" shouted the pig. "Not by the hairs of my chinny chin chin will I let a WOLF in! Put one paw on my house and I'll **huff**,

and I'll **puff**,

and I'll...."

"Hold it right there!" said the wolf. "This isn't YOUR house. It's the chickens' house."

"Who cares?" said the little pig. "Now go away—ALL OF YOU!"

What a horrid little pig he was.

Charming!

So the kind wolf invited all the chickens back to HIS house, which was built out of bricks and very strong indeed.

WOLF'S HOUSE

Meanwhile, the house built by the first horrid little pig...

was being eaten up by a herd of hungry cows.

The house built by the second horrid little pig...

was being pulled apart
by a flock of angry birds.

And the third horrid little pig . . .

Our NESTS!

You've taken our TWIGS!

was being pecked by
a rooster and went WEE WEE WEEEEEEEE EEEEEEE all the way back to
his brothers.

(Which was *just* what
the rooster wanted.)

Now NONE of the pigs had a home. But the wolf did. And it looked warm and cozy.

"This house would be perfect for us," said the horrid little pigs.

So they waited until dark.
Then they climbed onto the roof
and began to slide down the chimney.
The wolf heard the horrid little pigs, so he got out a
GREAT BIG POT OF BOILING...

WOLF'S HOUSE

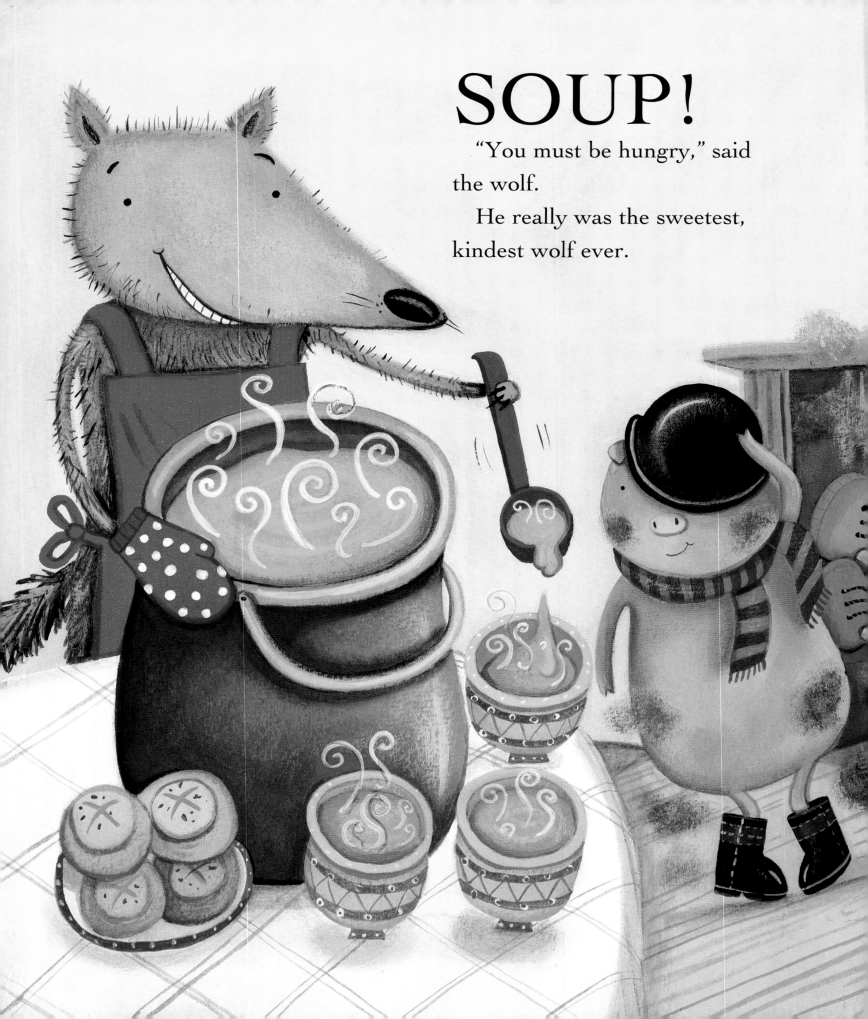

SOUP!

"You must be hungry," said the wolf.

He really was the sweetest, kindest wolf ever.

The friendly wolf let the pigs stay. And after a while, they stopped being lazy, horrid little pigs and learned how to build a sturdy house made of bricks...

which was big enough
for EVERYONE!

And they all lived
happily ever after.

The End

Liz Pichon

When Liz was little, she loved to draw, paint, and make things.
Her mom used to say she was very good at making a mess
(which is still true today!). She kept drawing and went to art school,
where she earned a degree in graphic design. She worked as a designer
and art director in the music industry, and her freelance work has
appeared on a wide variety of products. Liz is the author-illustrator of
several picture books and the award-winning Tom Gates series for older
children. Liz's books have won several prestigious awards, including
the Roald Dahl Funny Prize. Her books have been translated into
43 languages worldwide.